DATE DUE

Demco, Inc. 38-293

THE SMASHING SCROLL

BY MICHAEL DAHL
ILLUSTRATED BY BRADFORD KENDALL

Librarian Reviewer
Laurie K. Holland
Media Specialist (National Board Certified), Edina, MN
MA in Elementary Education, Minnesota State University, Mankato

Reading Consultant
Elizabeth Stedem
Educator/Consultant, Colorado Springs, CO
MA in Elementary Education, University of Denver, CO

 STONE ARCH BOOKS
Minneapolis   San Diego

151 Good Counsel Drive, P.O. Box 669,
Mankato, Minnesota 56002.
www.stonearchbooks.com

Library of Congress Cataloging-in-Publication Data
Dahl, Michael.
    The Smashing Scroll / by Michael Dahl ; illustrated by
Bradford Kendall.
    p. cm. — (Zone Books - Library of Doom)
    Summary: When the foul Spellbinder sends a giant scroll to
inprison the entire Earth, even the Librarian may be powerless to
stop its vast, unrolling page.
    ISBN-13: 978-1-59889-326-7 (library binding)
    ISBN-10: 1-59889-326-2 (library binding)
    ISBN-13: 978-1-59889-421-9 (paperback)
    ISBN-10: 1-59889-421-8 (paperback)
    1. Scrolls—Fiction. 2. Books and reading—Fiction.
3. Librarians—Fiction. 4. Fantasy. I. Kendall, Bradford, ill. II.
Title.
PZ7.D15134Sma 2007
[Fic]—dc22
2006027533

Art Director: Heather Kindseth
Cover Graphic Designer: Brann Garvey
Interior Graphic Designer: Kay Fraser

1 2 3 4 5 6 12 11 10 09 08 07

Printed in the United States of America

TABLE OF CONTENTS

The Library of Doom is the world's largest collection of strange and dangerous books. The Librarian's duty is to keep the books from falling into the hands of those who would use them for evil purposes.

CHAPTER 1

SMASH!

At the edge of a giant city, a **dark wind** blows through the fields. The breeze slips through an open window.

Two young brothers sit in their room, reading comic books.

One of the comics is called *Smash*.

The younger brother found it underneath his bed that night.

As he reads, the pages glow with a strange light.

The young boy gets a strange look on his face.

The boy stands up and curls
his comic book into a tight roll.
He bangs it against his hand.

Smack!

"What are you doing?" asks
his brother.

Smack!

A loud noise comes crashing
through the window.

〰〰 **Smash!** 〰〰〰〰〰

The boy drops the comic book.

Both boys run to the window
to see what caused the crash.

The boys live on a farm with
barns and sheds and silos.

One of the **tall** stone silos has crashed to the ground.

It rolls across the ground like a huge rolling pin.

As the boys watch, the silo smashes into the barn and crushes it **flat.**

CHAPTER 2

THE SCROLL

High above the countryside, the Librarian is flying. He is searching for the lost books of **the Library of Doom.**

The Librarian hears something crash far below. The sound waves smash through the sky.

The Librarian is hit.

He is knocked out by the powerful sound waves. He falls toward the ground.

Down, down, he is falling into the path of the rolling stone silo.

The silo smashes over trees and fences. It smashes through houses.

As it rolls forward, the silo leaves a trail of paper behind it.

The two boys see the Librarian's **dark shadow** hurtling down from the sky.

"He's falling toward that scroll," says the younger one.

"What do you mean, scroll?" asks his brother.

"I don't know," says the boy. "I just know that's what it is."

The Librarian's body is falling directly **in front** of the moving scroll.

Suddenly, he **stops.** The Librarian floats gently above the moving scroll.

The Librarian wakes up, still floating. Below him he sees letters written on a giant roll of paper. "The Scroll!" he says to himself.

CHAPTER 3

THE LAST STORY

The giant silo is really a scroll. As it smashes through the countryside, it unrolls its **magic page.**

People out walking at night are trapped by the giant covering of the scroll's page.

The two young boys can see where the scroll's page begins. It started when the scroll **smashed** through their barn.

"Look!" says the older brother. "It's a bunch of words."

"What is this all about?" asks the father.

"It's a story," says the younger brother.

The boys and their father read the words written at the top of the scroll's page. *The World's Last Story,* it says.

"How can it be the last story?" asks the older brother.

The Librarian still **floats** above the scroll's page.

He quickly reads the story. Now he understands the scroll's evil magic.

The scroll's story was written by a powerful wizard called the `Spellbinder`.

The Spellbinder was waiting for a person to read a special comic near the hidden scroll.

Then the scroll would **unwind** its magic page.

On and on the scroll would smash until the **whole world** was covered by its unrolling paper.

23

CHAPTER 4

THE CHASE!

The Librarian spreads his arms wide and rushes through the air.

Far ahead, the scroll is smashing cars parked along a lonely street.

Crunch! Smash!

A car is **turning a corner**.
Inside are a group of friends
coming from a birthday party.

The driver of the car sees
something strange in her mirror.

"What's that?" she yells.

Her friends look through the rear
window and see the scroll. One of
them **screams**.

"Hurry!" shouts her friend. "Go faster!"

The young woman pushes on the gas. The car **speeds** down the road.

"It's still coming!" yells a friend.

The scroll is moving faster, too.
Soon it will **crash** over the car.

The Librarian appears above the car. His boots **crunch** on the car's roof as he stands to face the scroll.

He reaches into his coat and pulls out a `small` book.

It reads *The World's First Story*.

The Librarian **throws** the book at the bottom of the scroll.

The book hits the bottom of the scroll. The scroll bounces up. It flies higher and higher. Its shadow passes across the moon, and then disappears.

The car squeals to a stop. The friends **pour** out of the doors.

"What happened?" they ask. "Where did that thing go?"

The driver looks at the roof of her car. She sees two prints where boots once stood. Then she looks up and sees a **shadow** pass across the moon.

THE END

A PAGE FROM THE LIBRARY OF DOOM

SCROLLS

A scroll is a piece of paper or parchment with writing on it, rolled up into a tube. Some scrolls are attached to a wooden rod or baton at either end. A scroll is read by unrolling the paper.

Scrolls can be read top to bottom, right to left, or left to right.

In Jewish synagogues, places of worship, the holy writings known as the Torah, are written on a scroll. Someone reads from the scroll during the worship service.

In China, artists paint on scrolls made of parchment and silk. The art of scroll painting is at least 4,000 years old!

In movies and television shows, the credits continually move across the screen. Viewers read the credits as if they were reading from an unrolling scroll. Now when writing moves across a screen, it is called *scrolling*.

ABOUT THE AUTHOR

Michael Dahl is the author of more than 100 books for children and young adults. He has twice won the AEP Distinguished Achievement Award for his nonfiction. His Finnegan Zwake mystery series was chosen by the Agatha Awards to be among the five best mystery books for children in 2002 and 2003. He collects books on poison and graveyards, and lives in a haunted house in Minneapolis, Minnesota.

ABOUT THE ILLUSTRATOR

Bradford Kendall has enjoyed drawing for as long as he can remember. As a boy, he loved to read comic books and watch old monster movies. He graduated from the Rhode Island School of Design with a BFA in Illustration. He has owned his own commercial art business since 1983, and lives in Providence, Rhode Island, with his wife, Leigh, and their two children Lily and Stephen. They also have a cat named Hansel and a dog named Gretel. Sometimes, they all sit together to watch an old monster movie.

GLOSSARY

hurtling (HUR-tuhl-ing)—falling or moving quickly

rolling pin (ROH-ling pin)—a long, round wooden tube used in baking for flattening dough

scroll (SKROHL)—a sheet of paper with writing on it wrapped into a tube shape

silo (SY-loh)—a tall, round building used for storing grain

spellbinder (SPEL-byn-dur)—a person who puts a spell on another

DISCUSSION QUESTIONS

1. Why do you think the Spellbinder used someone reading a comic book to start the smashing scroll?

2. Why do you think the Librarian was flying over the countryside? Do you think he knew something evil was about to happen? Explain.

3. The story on the giant scroll was called *The World's Last Story*. Why do you think it was called that? Who do you think wrote that story on the scroll?

WRITING PROMPTS

1. Imagine that you live on a farm next to the boys' farm. You wake up and see the giant scroll smashing through the countryside. Does it come near your house? What does it sound like? Describe what happens to you that night.

2. The Spellbinder is never shown in the story. Read carefully about the wizard (on pages 21 and 22) and you'll see we don't know if it is a man or a woman. What do you think the Spellbinder looks like? Write a description.

INTERNET SITES

Do you want to know more about subjects related to this book? Or are you interested in learning about other topics? Then check out FactHound, a fun, easy way to find Internet sites.

Our investigative staff has already sniffed out great sites for you!

Here's how to use FactHound:

1. Visit *www.facthound.com*

2. Select your grade level.

3. To learn more about subjects related to this book, type in the book's ISBN number: **1598893262**.

4. Click the **Fetch It** button.

FactHound will fetch the best Internet sites for you!